Lost Star

FanatiXx Publication
ISO 9001:2015 CERTIFIED

FanatiXx Publication

AM/56, Basanti Colony, Rourkela 769012, Odisha
ISO 9001:2015 CERTIFIED

Website: *www.fanatixx.in*

"Lost Star"

By: Imtiyaz Ahmad Shah

ISBN: 978-93-89923-55-1

Novella 1st Edition

Book Formatting: Saizal Gupta

Cover Design: Sagar Samal

Disclaimer

This is a work of fiction. Names, characters, places, and incidents are either the product of author's imagination or have been used illustratively and any resemblance to any person, living or dead, events or locales is entirely coincidental.

Imtiyaz Ahmad Shah asserts all rights to be identified as the author of this work.

Acknowledgement

This book is dedicated to my sublime and adorable parents: Mr. Mehboob Shah and Mrs. Mumtaza Begum.

To my lovable brothers: Mr. Aijaz Ahmad Shah and Mehraj-Ud-Din Shah.

To my sweet sisters: Shahida and Sumaya.

To my friends cum family: Syed Insha, Syed Iqra, Rashid Rafiq, Ezabir Ali, Akeel Peerzada, Dar Ishfaq, Sheikh Ishfaq, Humma Rashid, Bilal Ahanger, Ishfaq Parray, Aijaz Bhat, Amanpreet Kour, Jasmine, Sumaya Samad, Bilal Lone & Rafia Malla.

To my brilliant students: Muqadas Manzoor Roshangar, Humaira Ahad, Arizoo Shamim, Mahapara Aijaz, Nadeem Irshad, Mushtaq Khan, Bisma, Muskan, Masarat, Faiqa Ishtiyaq, Shariqa Mehraj, Kousar, Mehak, Musharaf Aijaz.

Author's Bio

The author of this book is from Kashmir and is presently the student of English Literature. The author has already written a book with the name, *The Caged Souls* and the book went viral among the readers. The author belongs to a small village of district Baramulla, named as Balhama Rafiabad.

Story of Mariah

It was the first time when she left her home in the middle of the snowy night without letting her family know about her departure.

"Where did she go?" asked Alee.

"She is lost somewhere in the dense snow-covered forests and that too, alone," responded Omar.

"What is that supposed to mean?" Exclaimed Alee.

"Let me explain," Omar replied.

Let's rewind what actually happened and what prompted her to leave her home and what were the consequences in the end. This story will unnerve you.

"Make sure you tell me the whole story," said Alee,

Let's start the journey.

Hold your breath for some time and listen to me. Listen carefully. No noise. No interruptions. Just listen to me only. No other side talks.

This story begins with Once Upon A Time, just like great stories do, of course. Now, lets us begin!

So, Once Upon A Time, in the deep dense forests, lived a poor family of the Gujjar tribes somewhere in Maidan Soz. They were living dreadfully and there was no source of earning and also there wasn't any kind of work that the head of the family could do to feed them.

They reared some animals and owned some land in which Abu Abad was seen working all day long, but that really was not enough to feed his family. Abu Abad worked hard in order to earn some bucks for their survival. He had one daughter namely Mariah and two sons Hamad and Ahmad. Hamad and Ahmad were school going kids and they had to travel some miles to reach the school.

"What about Mariah?" Said Alee.

"Well, Mariah, was the youngest among them and was very innocent," Replied Omar.

Abu Abad was a very roughshod and wicked person because he never let his family enjoy the moments of happiness. Though his love towards Hamad and Ahmad was immensely high; he used to treat his sons with great zeal and affection.

Abu Abad was a dual faced person as he always wanted to kill his only daughter Mariah and many a times when Mariah's mother was out, he tried to strangle his twelve-year-old innocent daughter with his bare hands.

"Why so?" Said Alee,

"Because he hated girl child; he had an opinion that girls are ominous and jinxed." Replied Omar,

"It is really sad how a father could try to kill his daughter?" mused Alee.

They lived in clay made shed with square shaped windows covered by some transparent sheets and there were some rusty iron rods hanging outside of the wall.

Abu Abad was a brave man besides his cruelty and he used to wake up whole night to protect his sons Hamad and Ahmad. Although the kids were all innocent and lovely, he still didn't like his daughter.

Their house was located in the center of a dense forest far from the village of Maidan Soz with their neighbors.

"Disgusting father." replied Omar, "He used to torture his wife and Mariah over useless things."

Abu Abad spends his day with his cattle and he used to carry Mariah with him to take care of his cattle. Though she was only twelve, yet Abu Abad forced her to do whatever pleased him. His reaction and behavior towards Mariah were as brutal as burning as a bullet. He many a times beat Mariah with the same sticks he used for his cattle.

"Brutal I would say," Alee said, "To torture a kid with bloody sticks is seriously a kind of homicide."

Abu Abad's wife was never given any kind of relief too. Like Mariah she too was suffering the torture. Her bruised thoughts were more painful than a wound in the rotten, alive and cursed heart. She had no one to share her pain with; she had no one to express her thoughts and tell her story to anyone who could console her inner disrupted peace.

Mariah never saw the love from her father and sometimes she used to shed her heart throbbing tears to make herself comfortable. She had only her victimized mother with whom she could share whatever was happening to her.

Mariah was seriously a beautiful kid with hazel eyes and silky straight brown hair. She used to wear a traditional red head-gear called Joji and it is a type of skullcap and over that skullcap was as usual their scarves locked at the top of the Joji. On the other side was a round shaped nose pin clipped on her nose at the right side. Her eyes and her melodious voice could intrigue anyone, but unfortunately that didn't melt her father Abu Abad.

"A man should never marry if he hates girl child. He should remain unmarried!" Alee exclaimed with anger, "ALLAH made us and He knew what He has to do. So, we are no one to suppress anyone whether it is transgender, girl or anyone else."

"Yes, you are right, but here Abu Abad has changed the whole scenario. He is doing what he likes and he is more than willing to kill his daughter, Mariah," Omar Replied.

Abu Abad was a seven-feet tall man with long twisted mustache coned at the end, that looks like a missile on the both sides is about to attack. He had reddish colored long hair and he used to wear an Afghani Cap which was famous and is still famous nowadays. His wrinkled face was as horrible as polluted as contaminated water. His fierce looks were life threatening not for Hamad and Ahmad, but for Mariah and her mother Huzaifa.

It was a conflicted family where every day was like a war for them and every night was like an uneasy hell. Huzaifa the mother of Mariah would cry in the night and hold her daughter Mariah in her arms to protect her from the brutal attacks of her father.

Abu Abad sold the famous ornaments of his wife Huzaifa and lost that in gambling. Gambling was his job besides raising cattle and beating his wife and daughter with crowbars was another job.

"Wasn't Mariah, going to school?" Questioned Alee.

"No, she was persecuted and she was told to stay at home; not actually at home, but to take care of cattle," replied Omar.

Abu Abad's desire was to raise his sons and that's why he admitted them in the nearby school of Maidan Soz. While on other side Mariah used to watch them going to school. She used to weep in the corner of her ripped house, her wish wasn't to raise the cattle, but to gain education as same as her brothers.

Her motive was different from her father and she always wanted to do creative activities. Though she was only twelve, yet mentally she was twenty-five. She never expressed anything and never raised a voice that could hurt her father. The only thing she wanted was to see her family happy, which wasn't at all. Torture, thrashing and beatings were a common activity for them. They didn't enjoy, but obviously her father does.

"Savage father of the century..." Alee said with a sigh.

Mariah's mother was a very pious lady. She never asked anyone for help, not even she asked her husband to fulfill her demands. Whatever she did... she did on her own. She had the capability to protect her family from any calamity and the first and foremost calamity was Abu Abad. She was a determined lady who kept herself busy in her work of handcrafts and pottery.

Huzaifa had long brown colored hair just like her daughter, twinkling eyes and round cheeks and she could fascinate anyone whosoever confronts her. She was a resilient lady and recovers any loss quickly, but she failed miserably to save Mariah, her adorable daughter. There was another member in their house namely Mukaram, Abu Abad's father. He was not well and was suffering from prolonged illness.

Mukaram, who was lying motionless on his broken bed spending his most of the time coughing and clearing his throat... He was suffering from asthma and many other untreated diseases. Mukaram met with an accident couple of years ago that left him bruised and unmoved. On the other side he was resting in such a room where cold and chilled nights had paralyzed his whole body. Despite the pain Huzaifa used to take a great care of her father-in-law. She never let him feel alone and deprived as he was deprived by his own son Abu Abad.

"Abu Abad, wasn't aware that he is doing wrong." Omar said.

"What kind of father and son he was?" Alee replied.

"He was neither a son nor a father because he never had a bit quality and respect for his family and most importantly for his sick father," Omar narrated.

Ok, let's have a cup of tea and we will taste the story. It will make our story tastier and touchier.

Mariah and Huzaifa both were greatly attached with each other, but they were not that much attached to Abu Abad. While as on the other side of the coin Hamad and Ahmad were also against his father for his brutality towards Mariah and Huzaifa, but who had thought they too would change in the end.

On one morning when Mariah left her home as advised by her savage father to take the cattle for grazing and take care of everyone whosoever comes with you. Mariah was distressed and teary she felt that this is the only job she had been assigned for. Mariah was outside leaned against the muddy wall of her house and her mother was watching her screaming loudly.

"May he die!" Huzaifa said and continued, "Oh, Allah, stop tormenting us we are no longer stout now."

A thick and heart wrenching tear trickled down from her eyes and she then wiped away to console herself. To make herself good again as she was the lady who never gave up.

"Male dominance since centuries has been a real headache in our societies. Our women folk never heave a sigh of relief as they are being treated as slaves," Alee expressed his concern.

"Yes, Alee, you are right and we ourselves are responsible for the mess we have caused. Despite the knowledge we still torment our women folk," Omar responded.

Mariah then left along with her cattle and took a deep breath and chanted, "May ALLAH rest my soul in peace."

She was in pain! Like other daughters are loved by their father she was horribly unloved and ill-treated one. She was a tormented daughter. She was prone to sufferings and drought like feelings. She was never admitted in any school like her brothers. Her ill-mannered father left her wounded and burned her desires.

"She should protest as we all have equal rights," said Alee.

"How could she? She was dependent like her grief-stricken mother," Omar replied.

In the mid of the day Mariah would watch school kids coming back from schools with bags tied at their back. She then cried and wept her tears. She then uses abusive words for her father. Mariah's whole day was consumed in pain and prolonged thoughts.

She used to return home along with her cattle at dusk when the light is yet to disappear and her mother would hug her and lift her into her arms to show love and affection as she never wanted to let her feel bad because of her father. Mariah then would go to her grandfather's room and hug him to cure his pain and to let him feel good.

Abu Abad never visited his father's room nor did he ask his wife about his condition. Mukaram was dying and Abu Abad was in wait for his death. He was in wait to bury his daughter and his sick father. There was no medicine available for Mukaram as he was in horrible pain.

Whenever Abu Abad returns from his work, he used to beat Mariah senselessly and without any reason. He would drag both of them by hair and on to a graveled and rough surface.

"Why he was doing all this?" questioned Alee.

"The reason was his loss in gambling. Whenever he lost something, he would recover his loss by beating his family and mostly, Mariah," Omar replied.

"Does it make any sense?" Alee asked angrily.

"It doesn't, but he was addicted to this!" replied Omar.

From the age of three Mariah suffered many back injuries and head injuries. Mariah was greatly terrorized by her cruel father.

"This is the world full of monsters and one among them was Abu Abad." Omar narrated in a low tune, "A father with such thoughts should be killed!"

"Yes, I am with this and everyone should be grateful if they have a daughter and daughters are as sacred as prayer." Expressed Alee.

Days passed with the same scene and with the same brute torture. Mariah was in depression to see her jubilant brothers going to school with their father holding their fingers on the both sides. She was un-loved by her father. The desires which were buried in her depressed heart were no longer available on the scene.

She had totally failed to recover what she had lost; her mother would convince her. She used to tell her stories of great daughters of the world who had witnessed the same... but they fought well to be on the top. She would sing songs for her and that would calm her soul.

The best mother! Mothers are always concerned about their children. They put their life at stake and save us from everything. We will never be able to understand the importance of mothers. It is rightly said that 'Heaven is under the feet of your mother'.

We are living in 21st century where everything is possible; where everything could be endured, but not discrimination and apartheid. Even in 21st century our girls are not safe. They are not able to stroll on the streets of their village; they are not able to get education; they are not able to participate in an event or any social activities. Maidan Soz was as dry as the end of monsoon showers. People belonging to that village had to suffer and they had to preserve their essential commodities for future use.

"Didn't, Mariah, raise her voice against her savage father?" Questioned Alee.

"No, she didn't," Omar replied, "She knew everything about her father. She never dared to utter a word that would bring out the wicked demon inside of him."

Oh, poor Mariah!

"It is so distressing and disgusting."

I have never seen a child who is actually terrorized by her father. This is brutal reality! Mariah never saw any hopes to flourish and blossom like the April flowers. After several months people were seen doing household chores and they were seen preparing themselves for the upcoming winter. But on the other side Abu Abad, was never so serious about such things. He took it lightly without knowing what consequences it could bring? Maidan Soz was covered with dense woods. So, we can expect anything; anything means anything.

"What preparations they had to make?" questioned Alee.

"Yes, some essential stuffs: rice, wheat, some dried vegetables, pulses, cereals and the skin of animals etc." replied Omar.

Throughout the summer season they had to dry up some green vegetables and preserve them for future use. Huzaifa prepared everything secretly without letting her husband know. She knew her careless husband would never come and help her in household chores.

It was a cursed story of a cursed mother and a cursed daughter and both were the victims of male dominance. In Maidan Soz schools get closed earlier than usual because they know snow and storm could come anytime. Winter season was so close and it was predicted that snow storm could create havoc and could bring curse in the village. Villagers were afraid!

"How they could predict?" asked Alee.

"They have witnessed it many a times." Answered Omar.

"This is the curse of innocent, Mariah, Isn't it?" Alee said.

"Not now, but it was snow storm which destroyed the hopes of Abu Abad," replied Omar.

"How?" Alee asked surprised at the fact.

"Just stay with me until this evening and get to know everything," Omar mumbled.

"Ok... just continue I am eager to know more."

Winter was just on the edge and Abu Abad's face had turned pale after he heard about the news of snow storm which was then broadcasted on the radio sets. He rushed here and there; he was in dilemma whether to do this or that. The sober Mariah saw her father doing the work and she went near him to help him out. But he slapped her face forcibly and asked her to leave him alone.

A deserted tear trickled down from her deep sunken tortured eyes and she went back into her tormented and confined den. The room she was staying was as same and horrible as the prison of 'Guantanamo' only she can console herself besides her mother.

Abu Abad was against the female folk. He was of the view that every male should dominate females, he used to treat his wife and daughter in the same way he had thought. This also shows that he hated not only his daughter, but every other daughter in his village. He was atheist who doesn't believe what rules we have been asked to follow.

Abu Abad was like a monster in human form that was always ready to destroy his family, but not Hamad and Ahmad. He used to shop for them; he used to get new clothes for them; love, warmth and everything was just made for Hamad and Ahmad. They were lucky, but not Mariah and her mother Huzaifa.

Mariah was given a room which was a bombarded place with ripped walls and peeled wall paint. The window was half broken and the quilt was more like a heap of decayed grass. It is obvious Mariah never saw any relief or solace since her childhood. Her finger nails had turned into something very horrible; many untreated wounds were clearly visible and her unkempt hair.

Mariah was much attached to her brothers and they all were good friends besides being brothers and sister. Abu Abad never wanted Hamad and Ahmad to play with Mariah, but whenever Abu Abad was out, they all used to assemble and play as if they had met after decades.

Brother, sister relationship is something very different from other relationships. Both brothers started an initiative to teach Mariah basics. They began to train Mariah so that she could not feel handicapped. Their perspective and ideology were very different than their ruthless father. They were utilizing their knowledge in a proper way. There wasn't any kind of ignorance and ego in them. Being polite and sober in nature was their basic and supreme goal towards success.

"So, there was only one barrier in between them and that was Abu Abad?" Alee Questioned.

"Yes, he was and I would say they were the most cursed and tormented family in Maidan Soz." Omar replied.

There was only a day left for schools and after that schools were supposed to get closed. Hamad and Ahmad decided to take Mariah to school as Abu Abad was out in the nearby meadows with his cattles. On the other side Huzaifa was preparing the sweet and pretty Mariah. She brought some new clothes for Mariah and decorated her unkempt and un-combed hair. She was just like the rays of morning sun; her eyes were as striking as the afternoon heat. She was another moon belonging to another planet.

Huzaifa tied up a black thread in her left hand as it will protect her from evil eyes. Both were engrossed in each other's gaze and Huzaifa would kiss her forehead and hug her tightly to give her sense of satisfaction, but inside they were both dead. The gong bell ringed loudly and the entire trio left for school. They were happy as if it was another 'Eid' for them.

The amaranthine smile on her lips was just like the scene of moon and stars playing with each other without knowing their worth. But who had thought that this smile would no longer be visible on her lips; who had thought that Mariah would never go to school again; who had thought Mariah would never smile again.

"What happened? I mean I'm not able to understand." Alee again questioned surprisingly,

"Someone belonging to the same village conveyed the news to Abu Abad and he told him about, Mariah," Omar replied.

Abu Abad got infuriated and his ferocious eyes were signaling that something bad is going to happen. After hearing this incident, he cut short his trip and brought his cattle back to the village and went straight to the school with his old and upturned stick called 'Lathi'.

He was angry over the decision made by Hamad and Ahmad. After some minutes he stormed into the school through the gate and went straight to that class where Mariah was sitting and studying with her brothers. The teacher was teaching them and suddenly the door was hardly struck by Abu Abad. A loud collective shriek came out of the class and it echoed everywhere.

When Mariah saw her savage father, she went slowly to the corner and bowed down her head inside her arms, but she failed miserably to save herself. Even teacher couldn't do anything to save Mariah. Abu Abad grabbed Mariah by hair and dragged her out of the class and onto the ground.

The teacher tried to save Mariah even Abu Abad didn't spare him and he slapped him right on his face. Mariah was ruthlessly beaten up by her father, but nobody came forward to save her from her inhuman father. He did the same with Huzaifa and the beatings were so terrible that they couldn't move from their places. Their swollen faces, fingers, eyes, and scar full back denoted that how brutal Abu Abad was.

On the other side Mukaram who was looked after by Huzaifa was motionless and he too couldn't do anything. He remained hungry for three days as both Mariah and Huzaifa were not able to do any kind of work.

Abu Abad was pitiless and there wasn't any kind of humanity inside his dead and rotten heart. He was as same as the stone that doesn't have feelings or emotions, but when it gets derailed it can kill anyone whosoever comes in its way.

"I am confused whether to call him human or wild feral animal." Alee expressed his concern while wiping away his withered crimson colored tears.

"He was neither human nor any animal because animals do have feelings. They can understand a bit if not the whole. He was something very different," Omar replied, "Bring some food I'm hungry."

"Yes, give me ten minutes I will be back soon." Replied Alee.

After waiting ten minutes the food was served.

"It is tasty, really!" Omar said.

"My mom prepared this. So, how it could not be tasty." Replied Alee.

"Your mom is great. May she live long."

"So, how Mariah and Huzaifa survived after such brutal attack?" Alee Questioned.

It was Almighty Allah who saved them, but was really not enough to get rid of. Many a times Mariah told her mother to run away from this land of demons. She told her mother that she cannot face any hardships; she cannot tolerate more torture.

Huzaifa know that Mariah has now become weak due to the heinous acts of her father Abu Abad. She kept shedding tears all day long and night. Her nights sometimes disappear with sleeplessness and echoes of her screams. Those clamorous screams could be still heard in the valleys of Maidan Soz.

"What do you mean by this? Alee questions.

"Yes, people still hear those screams whenever they travel into dense woods," Replied Omar.

"How is this possible?" Alee surprisingly questioned again.

"Just listen and wait."

On that historical day Abu Abad kept Mariah outside his bloody prison. She had to tolerate the chilled breeze and the scare of night. Indeed, it was not a good sign for Mariah. Mariah was stammering, shivering in the cold. Huzaifa tried to get her child back, but she was not allowed by her husband.

He told Huzaifa to let Mariah die in the cold; let the cold freeze her nerves; let the horrible night squeeze her heart; let the animals break all her bones; let the insects decay her body. The disquieting night passed with the hope to rise again.

Huzaifa didn't sleep for a single moment while Abu Abad was eagerly waiting to see the dead body of Mariah. But what happened next was unbelievable; even Abu Abad was puzzled to see Mariah better than usual. She was sleeping as if the invisible quilt had come from heaven only for Mariah. It looked as if wind had turned its face away from Mariah; it looked as if fairies had come to chant sleep inducing tales for Mariah.

Huzaifa had never thought that Mariah could survive, but we are humans and Allah is always with us and He can destroy anyone who does injustice with other innocent people. Abu Abad was confused as how to show his ridiculous face to little Mariah. He was the Pharaoh in the form of Abu Abad.

"See, she is an angel," Alee said in low tune with a sigh.

"Yes, she was. Most importantly Abu Abad was ashamed of himself. He was regretting what he has done with this little kid," Omar replied.

"So, finally he understood the worth of a girl child," Alee questioned.

"No, not yet... he was about to face the wrath of nature," Replied Omar angrily.

On one evening, all were set to have the dinner, but Mariah wasn't there. She was outside playing with little chickens and puffy kittens. Probably she was happy with them, for her they were her family. Mariah knew she had no value in her family. She only adores her mother who always stands by her side. While having dinner Huzaifa told Abu Abad to remain alert as it has been predicted heavy snowfall this season.

"This is a rumor," he ended his statement with sluggish and obnoxious statement. Mariah was hungry from couple of days as she used to drink water to survive, but her desire was now to end herself. She was only waiting for the perfect moment to tell her family that girls are not burden for their families.

"Was she thinking about committing suicide?" Alee said,

"Kind of, but she failed many times. Sometimes she was saved by her mother and the spiritual leader 'Imam' of that village," Answered Omar.

The phobias are still in our societies and they dwell somewhere in our dead hearts. Not only Abu Abad, but other men folks of the valley took active part in such activities: Like earning money by different modes of labor etc. They had terrorized the whole village by their violent acts.

They had snatched the basic rights of women and they treat them as slaves. Slavery hasn't yet ended as it was proclaimed some centuries ago. I still remember Abraham Lincoln who fought bravely to end the menace and torment over the weaker sections of the societies. We have failed to do the same; we should give the same rights to women as they too deserve applause in each and every field.

They are not different from us, but they are unique in every way. We never see our mistake, but notice every bit about them and began to enquire. That is why I think we should end male dominance as it could ruin the essence of societies.

The day is not far when women come out of their dens and protest like lionesses and that time, we may get weak and we have to accept our defeat. The phase of life they had been through was like spending some minutes in the hell fire.

Chapter 2

In the mid of the night snow began to fall at a great pace. It looks as if the prediction was right, but regarding it as 'rumor' Abu Abad had never thought that his rumor could become reality. In winter season everything gets interrupted and disrupted due to the blockage of roads, communication, damaged electricity poles, lines etc. people have to suffer this torment for at least three months. Due to heavy snow people may suffer dearth of essential stuffs and with a massive terror inside people of Maidan Soz were perplexed, scared and furious as how to cope up with this unbearable and threatening snow blizzard. Prayers, discussions and everything was on the cards to save themselves and their families from this hazardous time that has turned into curse for them.

It was the 'Fajr' time when Imam called for Salah and people were seen rushing towards the nearby mosque. The purpose to offer Salah was only to overcome the stress of ongoing snow storm. The fact is that they never offered Salah there and it was the first that they began to visit mosques and worship there.

The holy places too remained closed since decades. It was probably a curse wandering and making them restless. Everybody realized that one should not forget ALLAH as He is Omnipotent and Omnipresent. He is present everywhere and is watching us keenly and observing what we are doing without having the fear of Almighty ALLAH. People were terrorized and they tuned to the radio stations for more updates; the side talkers were abusing, cursing weathermen and someone said, 'It is happening all because of the weathermen.'

Ha-ha!

"How could he be the one behind all this?" Alee said with a sarcastic smile on his lips.

"As I have told you that they had no sense where to talk and what to talk." Replied Omar.

Women folks and kids were not allowed to come out from their respective houses. Time passed and people were stuck onto their radio sets staying in touch with news updates. In fact, this undeniable truth had unnerved everyone. Anger, fear had left a massive impact on their minds and they kept praying all day long. They kept themselves busy in different kind of activities. Their source of earning was shut for months.

Now, they had to stay at home without any work to do. It is a serious threat for such nations where a capable person is not able to do the work which he needs to do. However, people had firm faith in ALLAH; they knew the powers and what ALLAH can do. He is the destroyer and creator of the universe. We should be satisfied whatever decision He is going to make. We have lost our insight; faith and we have been diverted from the right path by Satan.

As the 'Fajr' time passed and little light breezed in; due to the snowfall the whole valley and mountains were capped with the white curtains of the gleaming and glittering snow; those plaintive calls of 'Koels'. Chirping and gossiping of other birds and some other could be seen gliding high up in the sky. Everyone was busy in shoveling the snow off from their roofs and many others were engaged in clearing the roads. Mariah was still asleep. Many a times Huzaifa tried to wake her up, but she didn't even respond.

"Not responded?" Alee questioned, "Was she dead?"

Ha-ha!

"No, she wasn't, but she pretended to be dead."

Huzaifa was scared and she began to scream. Everyone rushed into the room where Mariah was sleeping and pretending to be dead. Abu Abad smiled to hear the news and went away. He was happy inside to see his daughter dead. Initially he thought that his dream came true, but it was all a lie and hoax.

Mariah was trying to see the reaction of her father, but the reaction was heart breaking. When she woke and she told everyone about the truth that she was lying. Huzaifa opened up her arms and hugged Mariah tightly and said, "Don't dare to leave me alone."

Huzaifa was shedding hopeless tears for Mariah and there was unending anger for Abu Abad. Huzaifa and Mariah never heaved a sigh of relief ever in their life.

"How could a father think badly about his daughters?" Alee expressed his concern.

"If we talk about past, I have read many books regarding the same. At that time girls were buried alive as their parents consider them ominous and burden. Same was happening with Mariah and the tormentor was Abu Abad," Answered Omar.

Both Huzaifa and Mariah were in tears and they were in dilemma whether to choose death over this disrespectful life they were leading. They thought that it is better to live in hell than this planet where girls are considered as burden. The history was repeating and this time what will go down in history was the story of innocent and suppressed Mariah and her mother Huzaifa. Abu Abad was so cruel that he didn't even spare his motionless and paralyzed father Mukaram. Huzaifa too was beaten up mercilessly because she tried to save the old Mukaram.

"How about snow and did any storm hit the valley?" Alee questioned while taking off his jacket and hanging it to the wall.

"Yes, snow storm almost ruined the little valley of Maidan Soz." Omar replied.

You know it takes long months and months to get the road cleared and sometimes years to rectify electricity. Snow could cause massive interruption in such fields and most of the time villagers of Maidan Soz remain disconnected from essential commodities. Maidan Soz was a deprived village.

Government officials pay their visit only when they need their valuable votes.

They would console them with the hoax that their needs would be fulfilled, but when they become the rulers they get disappeared for years and years. This was not only happening with this village, but many other tribes were in the same mess. People belonging to that village were less literate. Now, they were trying to teach their boys, not girls as they hate them more than anything else.

Their faith was as fragile as the flower 'Touch Me Not' but they were on the wrong track living with the thought that they would get success in doing so. People of Maidan Soz were more ignorant and less intellectual. At times Abu Abad threatened Huzaifa and asked her to leave his house and sign on the divorce papers. Huzaifa never was able to get control over Abu Abad as she was growing weak.

Divorce!

"How could he do like that?" Alee asked completely shocked at the revelation.

"He was more like animal than human. He forcibly did this to get rid of from Huzaifa and Mariah. He knew Huzaifa would never leave Mariah alone," Omar replied lowering his head in shame.

Abu Abad was well aware about the love between Mariah and Huzaifa. Only one thing was pinching his soul was the rested body of old Mukaram. He was waiting for his death after that he may feel the relief.

"So, only three people were confined and terrorized," Alee said.

"Yes, and they were Huzaifa, Mariah and Mukaram," Answered Omar.

Mariah was the reason for all this. If Mariah hadn't been there things would have been better. Maybe he could have accepted Huzaifa and Mukaram willingly. He may care for them and he may do all the work for them, but barrier was created by Mariah.

Although she wasn't that kind of daughter, yet she suffered the most. She suffered many horrible summer solstices like years. Her dream to become doctor was shattered; her dream was to provide the basic education to its people. She was the different child in the whole Maidan Soz. She was gifted, but ALLAH chooses the wrong person for this prestigious gift. He doesn't deserve a daughter like Mariah.

"ALLAH is never wrong in His decisions and He knows what is wrong and what is right," Alee said while nodding his head.

"Yes, but here the story is pretty different and incomparable," Answered Omar.

"How?"

"Just listen," Replied Omar.

Abu Abad never knew that he is harboring sins and he is giving more preference to his sons and less, even nothing to Mariah. He was engrossed in his own self-made dreams which were only meant to be broken. He was stone-hearted fellow; he liked his cattle more than his daughter Mariah.

Chapter 3

"God has created us equally and we should abstain from those things which could lead us to destruction," Said the Imam on Friday prayers.

Imam was the most spiritual and spirit expeller in the village. He was not from Maidan Soz, but somewhere else. He told them that God has never done any injustice with anyone in this paradise like planet. It is we who have done the massive destruction even after many warnings and natural calamities. He was of the view that one day we all have to face the wrath of Almighty Allah and we will then have no answer and no good deeds to represent ourselves in front of ALLAH.

"Does he know anything about Mariah?" Alee questioned.

"Yes, he does," Answered Omar, "He tried to resolve the issue, but it was all in vain."

He enquired and then advised Abu Abad not to beat Mariah as she is the child of heaven and she doesn't know anything. But he didn't even listen to his true words.

Alas! Had he lend his ears to what Imam said things would have been different? He was ignorant so was his ideologies and false belief. Huzaifa was somehow running her house and taking care of Mukaram and Mariah. She had left her dead hopes and she knew things would never change it will only get worse and worse in the future.

She had that capability to defeat any kind of human calamity because humans are nowadays wilder than the animals of the haunted forest. Days passed by no one knew that Maidan Soz is going to face a massive and catastrophic destruction.

"What do you mean?" Alee questions.

"Yes, you heard it right," Omar replied.

Maidan Soz witnessed the most destructive snow avalanche after almost a century. Earlier the villager felt some jerks, but they ignored it intentionally. It was the fourth wintry day, chilled and ice like solid. Four feet snow was recorded earlier, but it was not a threat.

 Maidan Soz was itself a mountain, but it was mountain within in mountain. So, there was always threat of land sliding, snow skidding and the same happened there. Apart from Abu Abad's house he owned a closed shed far from his house approximately half a kilometer from where he kept his domestic animals' worth lacs.

In the middle of the night the whole valley was cordoned by snow and everything looked deserted. There wasn't any kind of sound made by animals nearby. Whole village was in deep slumber; Abu Abad and Mariah both were feeling restless. There was some kind of confusion in their minds and something very bad was going to happen!

Abu Abad woke up and opened the door of his room and saw there was nothing outside except the little snowflakes and a strong breeze. He ignored and went back to his bed where he was lying curved with his head up supported by his right hand and he kept his eyes open for a while, but it didn't last for long. Eventually he closed his eyes and slept and heard a deep sigh with hoarse cough. The regular coughing of Mukaram was not letting him sleep properly often times he scolded him, but it was not enough. He felt the restlessness of the dark night with monsters around. He had nightmares and many times he opened and closed the door.

"Was it the curse of Mariah?" Alee asked.

"Might be, but can't say what that was?" Omar replied.

At sharp 2 O'clock Abu Abad heard some noise and he went up hurriedly and went straight to the mountain side window. When he opened the window there was nothing visible, but the sound of skidding snow. He was pained and he rushed towards the door; opened it and went outside. The scene shocked him as the snow avalanche was approaching towards Maidan Soz and straight towards his shed.

"Oh God! You mean snow avalanche banged the valley," Alee again questioned.

"Yes, but not the whole only part of it," Omar replied.

Abu Abad was screaming clamorously for some minutes, but nobody was listening to his screams and pleas until the avalanche ruined and destructed half of Maidan Soz. His hard work of beating Mariah paid off. His whole shed was inside the avalanche.

Oh God!

"Poor, Abu Abad," Alee said.

"Well, Abu Abad was in tears, but nobody had any kind of information regarding the same until morning turn into mourning," Replied Omar.

Horrible though!

"Yes, Indeed."

Everyone, even a kid rushed towards the spot, but they found nothing except the rubble of dead animals. Abu Abad had never thought that this could happen with him. He never paid attention towards this and kept beating Mariah and Huzaifa. They too have hearts, feelings and sentiments... they also want to stroll freely.

We are still not given freedom and we are still suffering like the slaves of 18th century.

"Didn't anyone visit the spot?" Alee questioned.

"No one did, but Abu Abad kept visiting there to shed his never revealed tears," Omar responded.

He was never able to forget his loss. The interest he had in rearing domestic animals was also lost and there wasn't any reason for him to live again. He couldn't bear the massive loss. After many days villagers took a step to clear the rubble and erect a new shed for Abu Abad, but he was not willing to do it again. He willingly refused to do the same.

"You told me Mariah was also feeling restless at that time. What is the connection between? Why was she not sleeping?" Alee expressed his concern.

"The reason is clear daughters love their father more. Despite the torture Mariah doesn't want to see her father in pain and despair," Omar replied.

"What a great child."

"Yes. Indeed she was!" Omar exclaimed.

Abu Abad remained hungry for weeks and he was forced to take the food, but refusal was the only answer people got from him. He fixed his place outside his house and kept thinking about his loss. It was indeed a big loss and there wasn't any kind of source to recover the loss.

Sometimes he would return home late and sometimes he wouldn't. There was chaos every side and every side was surrounded by confusion and pain. On the other side Mukaram was getting worse day by day due to the less availability of medicines. Medicines were more important for him to survive and to live again. But scene was different and story took another shape.

Another shape!

"What do you mean?" Alee questioned.

"Yes, now the style Abu Abad was living with has risen to new heights." Omar replied.

"I am puzzled," Alee said, while scratching his forehead.

"Let's take a step forward," Answered Omar.

Abu Abad was confused as what to do and what not to. He adapted many ways to get back what he had lost. He took many steps, changed many ways so on... but it all went in vain. His hatred for Mariah was growing more and more. He had become half-crazy and it looked the wandering souls of his cattle was inside haunting him. His fierce eyes were looking like he is going to attack anytime and anyone whosoever comes into his way. Little Mariah was innocent by thoughts she was still thinking that his father is lovable and he loves her more than anything.

On one pleasant morning with the chirping of birds Mariah went out from her room and she was looking blankly at the sky. She was fascinated with the scene as how these crystal clear snowflakes fall on the earth and cover it with the white shining curtains. She was lost in the nature, creation and sometimes past thoughts and moment could pinch her heart and she felt pain inside.

She was twelve and her thoughts yet ideology was twenty-five. Sometime she would talk with the passing wind, touch it and feel it. Sometimes she would scream aloud calling the angels of heaven. Sometimes she would call the other Mariah to come and play with her. She would go into the snow-covered fields and play like angels in the heaven. She was itself an angel who has come from a distant land.

Sometimes she would sing songs of love 'Ballads' and sometimes 'An Ode'. Her sufferings were different from the sufferings of other creatures. She loved the little echo she would make while screaming her name loudly. In a little breeze her hair would blossom like the yellowish flowers of mustard fields. Mariah was a gifted child and Abu Abad was an unlucky father who kept beating her. He realized it a little later.

After sometime Abu Abad was recovering slowly and he was able to overcome the trauma he was suffering from. He was stable now and now he could do the work again. Huzaifa was happy to see him again in his past form. Now, she was thinking that the incident might have changed his rustic and uncivilized thoughts. But she was wrong in fact Abu Abad had become fiercer than he was in past. He was like an injured lion roaming madly in the jungle.

Now, his next torture and target was Mariah. In fact, he put the whole blame of Mukaram's accident over Mariah. He told her that she is ominous and she brought the curse in his house. Firstly, Mukaram met with an accident then the snow avalanche destroyed his shed. He was playing the bloody game against Mariah, but he crossed the limits and boundaries of cruelty. On one painful night he found that everyone is sleeping and he made a plan to kill Mariah by strangling her neck or putting the pillow over her head. Such dreadful thoughts were roaming inside his filthy mind and if he succeeds, he would feel the relief he was searching for years. He tried many times, but he failed miserably to kill Mariah.

"Brutal father he is," Alee said with tears in his eyes.

Mariah's presence never let him do his work; he was not able to control himself from killing his daughter. Oftentimes he used to stay out from his home for days and whenever he comes back Mariah was the target. When Mariah learned to recover her depression Abu Abad would come again to take her where she was, the initial stage of depression. So, here Abu Abad's motive was to kill Mariah by killing her emotions and feelings.

Chapter 4

Despite all that Mariah still loved her father, but she never knew it would take her precious life. Her scars were never filled again, her sunken deep eyes with dark circles around were looking more coal balls then eyes. After that cruel and destructive winter people of Maidan Soz began to start their work again. But for Mariah every winter, summer, spring and autumn was extremely cruel.

Now, she loved to live her life happily without letting anyone know that she is feeling unbearable pain inside her broken heart. She had forgotten everything what had happened with her and what is going to happen in future. She concentrated on present and she thought that it is only present who could make us happy at any moment.

Schools re-opened again and the jolly kids were seen rushing towards their school among them were brothers of Mariah. I have read the poem of T.S Eliot 'The Waste Land' where he wrote the first line of the poem as 'April is the cruelest month' I agree with that because April was seriously a cruel month for Mariah.

The cruel incense of April was making her restless sometimes she would go up to the roof top of her house and watch at the school going kids walking hand in hand with each other and the smile on their lips was killing her inside.

Her desire was to get the education and become the doctor, but it was shattered by her father.

"Why on earth was this happening to her?" Alee exclaimed.

"Don't know why, but we can't change the nature of human," Responded Omar.

"Girls are assets for any nation then why we act like beasts?" Alee expressed his concern.

"Because we are not aware and we are acting like animals and animal do not have that sense to cope up with problems," Omar replied.

The flow of tears was persistent and it refused to stop. Even though Mariah tried to hide her pain, but she failed to not express it. She was never given liberty, but she was given liberty in staying at home within the walled boundaries of her cruel prison.

"May Almighty ruin his ego and hatred towards Mariah," Alee said with low tune.

Amen!

And same happened with Abu Abad. Mariah couldn't endure to watch her brothers going to school so she preferred to stay with cattle instead of watching them. Those meadows, woods, bubbly buoyant sounds, clear streams, birds, echoes, mountains and many other things attracted Mariah and she began to love them. She used to wake up and visit as early as possible. She had almost forgotten everything about past. She had lost the touch with pain and she was much attached to nature than her family.

Huzaifa felt very happy to see her daughter in a good mood from dawn till dusk. She did every household chore happily without knowing that she wasn't made for this, but she thought that helping her mother could release some sort of stress. Now, Mariah was able to understand what they are actually made for... they are made to get married!

Yes, it is truth, but we can't suppress their dreams. They too want to touch the skies, so why torture them without knowing their worth.

As the time passed Mariah was happy with her life and she was now twenty one. Now, she was more beautiful than usual. Her striking eyes could fascinate anyone and her melodious voice was a perfect bliss. One could easily dwell in her eyes and voice. She was a never written poetry and maybe it was for someone who could love her immensely. From twelve to twenty one Abu Abad made numerous plans to kill her daughter, but he failed to impress his blind heart. Mariah was still unloved and Abu Abad never spoke to her with love.

"I feel sorry for her," Alee said, "How about Mukaram?"

"Mukaram died when Mariah was sixteen due to unavailability of medicines," Omar replied.

"Oh, may Allah rest his soul in peace."

Abu Abad was happy because Mukaram was no longer visible. So, one barrier was gone and the other one was waiting. Mukarams' death was not natural, but a pre-planned murder. On the other side both the brother's of Mariah went to the city for further education. Now, they were mature kids, but unfortunately, they were same as their father.There were many similarities in them and they began to treat their mother badly when they finished their studies and came back to the village.

It was thought that they would come up with good knowledge, but they came up with so many ill ideas. Well, Abu Abad was happy to see his sons ascending his bloody throne. Mariah was lost in nature. She could wander the whole Maidan Soz alone. People began to like her and they forget that she is the daughter of cruel Abu Abad. Kids used to play with her and there was happiness all around. But her father never wanted to see his daughter doing such activities with other people belonging to the same village.

The level of cruelty risen again and he told Mariah to not visit again in the nearby woods. He told his sons to keep an eye on Mariah and not to let her go out from her room. She was again captivated and the happiness she was living with was no longer on the map.

The old little Mariah appeared again and there wasn't any kind of way out for her to come out from this complexity. Somehow she had forgotten everything about the past, but her father made her slave again. The dream Huzaifa had watched decades ago to see her sons getting the highest ranks was also broken because they don't deserve to be there.

"Why only women suffer even after all hardships and hard work?" Alee asked.

"It is because we don't have much knowledge about how to treat a woman in our society. We only know how to make them slaves forever. We left no stone unturned to play with their emotions," Omar replied.

No religions in the world permits us to take the bad advantage of woman. They have high status in our society; they can stroll freely; they can make friends; they can teach; they can get the education. So, we don't have any right to snatch their basic rights.

Sometimes Huzaifa would cry out some painful verses from her heart because apart from Abu Abad, her sons also began to torture her. They forget that she was their poor mother who holds them in her womb for nine months; who hold their finger to teach them how to talk and walk. Now, they forget everything.

To Whom Shall I Tell My Grief

It was the time when I dreamt for you,

When you were playing gently in my proud womb...

You were whispering calmly and I remember that,

At that time, I rewrote my fate for you my dearest sons...

I always used to smile when I was in labor pain,

How harrowing that pain was you never knew my

dearest sons...

I ignored those pains, but instead I kept waiting for you,

And when you were born every pain washed away with

your angelic innocence...

I always felt unrest and sleepless through the nights,

Because you didn't sleep without my efforts and care...

My dearest sons my hardships turned into blessing just

because of you,

I always did my best to make you happy and peaceful...

My sons I am that mother who holds you finger for your

first footsteps,

Who taught you the first word 'Ma' and slowly you learn

to lisp 'Ma'...

You remember those moment you were doing before
every meal,
And your immeasurable desire for fairytales and lullabies
before going to bed...

I always guarded you whenever you were in grief and
discomfort,
I gave you everything and never made you feel worse...
Whenever I found you in grief I felt worried and that
was my love,
Oh, my dearest sons you saw external smile, but not pain
and sorrow...

Now, I am growing old and tearfully helpless and lonely,
Your dishonesty left me mopping in chilly and dark
nights...
My dearest son what deleterious reward is this for all my
sacrifices,
Yes! Yes! Burden I am as you feel... to whom shall I tell
my grief?

These painful verses came out from Huzaifas' heart for her disobedient and dishonest sons. Mother's sacrifice and in return they get nothing.

"How horrible I can feel the pain inside," Alee said in a startled voice.

"Even I can feel her pain, but we can only regret in the end after attempting sins," Replied Omar.

"I still cannot believe! Such things still exist in our so-called peaceful world," Alee said.

Huzaifa was not much old as she appeared the pain she was suffering from had ruined her inner peace and the fair complexion she once had in her youthful days. Abu Abad was still stout, strong and full of energy because he never cared about his family. He kept doing those activities which were against the norms of the society. Rules were not made for him he thought, but in return he created rules and let his family follow those self-made filthy rules.

Chapter 5

There was a place named as Murray in Maidan Soz. It was an attractive place where people from different parts of the country used to visit once in a year. There were some antique mannequins and streams of different shape and size and through these streams a different kind of water kept flowing. People were much fascinated towards this place. Travelers, writers and some other people of different mindset used to visit Murray for personal satisfaction because there was calmness in everyside. Murray looked much different from Maidan Soz.

Mariah's favorite place was Murray there she used to sing songs aloud. She was in love with that place. The greenery, brownie woods with dense boughs, those plaintive calls of birds and mountains attracted her most. She long to get lost in those woods where she found the peace and love of her life!

"Love... What does it mean?" Alee exclaimed.

"Yes, she fell in love with the nature and with that guy who used to visit Murray," Answered Omar.

"Who was he?"

"He was an ardent lover, writer and poet."

"It is interesting! Tell me his name and how did he find Mariah?" Alee said,

As I told you Murray was an attractive place, but Mariah was more enchanting than Murray. So, no one would be able to control his feelings after encountering that beautiful flower. His name was Samar who had come from distant land. He was writer and he was in Murray for the same purpose, writing. Having said that Murray is the best place for writers and artists it has those special features where one could feel peace and serene.

"So, how did they meet?" Alee questioned.

"It was a strange meeting it felt like Kais met Leila," Replied Omar.

So, strange was their story! Samar had come for his educational tour and besides that he used to visit alone for his novel, but he never knew that the novel he is going to pen down would be about his love and him. He was in search of someone who could impress his soul and who could stole his heart at the first sight. His long pending request was about to complete and his love story was on the edge to create another conflict.

"Tell me how did they meet?"

"Have patience brother you will get to know about it soon," Omar replied.

On one morning Mariah visited Murray to get herself out of depression and family stress. She went straight to that tree where she loved to sit and started leaning against it. She stared blankly at the bold mountains standing tall, guarding the dainty villages of Maidan Soz and Murray. The sun spread its rays through the gaps of crisscrossed hills as it rose slowly; soaking the sky in shades of scarlet and soft orange. Birds flew across, heading towards their jobs. From dawn till dusk Murray never lost its beauty and charm. It kept calling people to visit again and again.

A tear rolled down from her cheeks and her heart felt heavy with confusion and sadness. She was in grief since the dawn of her life. Now, she sometimes visits Murray and shed an ocean of tears to release her stress. But she was unaware about what is going to happen next. On the same day and same morning Samar went to search his inner peace in the valleys of Murray. And he started his journey with this beautiful poem about the scenic beauty of Murray.

Hold thy breath...

Close thy eyes, and see the delicacy around,

Touch it, feel it, taste it, and hear how it sound.

The divinity in the vernal breeze seems heaven,

And the serene in the solitary field seems haven.

Wander the earth, and its appealing grace,

Feel it's tempting attributes, and begin the race.

Fill thy dawn with the lusty love of birds singing,

Listen to them, and appreciate what they are bringing.

At night; ye look at the glimmering and gleaming stars,

It looks as if they have ended up the millions old wars.

Those magnificent elevations, rivers, oceans and streams,

They fall, and sink; they descend and rise; like our
dreams.

Feel yourself up, and have a good time with alluring
nature,

Talk to birds, trees, mountains, and make it your culture.

"Wow! This is something very unique," Alee said surprisingly and began to enquire more.

"Apart from his writings, he was also an interesting person with wonderful thoughts inside," Omar replied.

He was roaming in the woods of Murray and kept observing things around. He would walk miles and miles to get his story that was not far now. It was closer than it appeared; he never forgets the habit of carrying his dairy and a pencil to write every bit about the places where he visits. He kept walking through the forests and he kept writing what fascinates him. While walking he heard some whispering it looked as if someone was crying. He approached and saw Mariah; he was stuck and dumbstruck to see her beauty.

Mariah was looking down and she didn't realize that someone is watching her. Samar too felt heavy as if he had found a gem. He hid himself behind the pine tree and kept staring at Mariah. He had not only found his story, but at that moment he fell in love with her. Suddenly, Mariah felt a gentle and familiar touch on her right shoulder and she was startled out of her thoughts.

She turned around slowly to find herself looking into Samar's soft hazel eyes, his dark hair framing his fair skin and ever so mesmerizing smile made her feel at ease all at once. Both exchanged their never met gaze; they were lost in each other's gaze. They felt the music of love in the background and those angels around them playing the chores. Samar couldn't control his fingers from wiping away glistering tears on her cheeks.

Mariah could hear his heart beating rhythmically and she felt that she had found her soul mate. After exchanging gaze both disappeared in a jiffy and Mariah kept running as fast as she could; her hearts beats were faster than she could ever think. She was not able to breathe, not even able to stop her steps. She was quivering, stammering and trembling. On the other side Samar was lost and he took the refuge somewhere in the woods. He began to write his novel with the title 'Anonymous Love' and the first line was...

"And then I saw her angelic face it seemed as if she had come from the heaven. She was so beautiful than the soft brightness of moon under the clear sky."

Now, his habit of visiting the meadows of Murray never stopped and he never restricted himself to explore more about Mariah. For some days, Mariah didn't visit her favorite place because she was not in a position to get there. She kept thinking about Samar profoundly and she used to suffer disquieting nights. She was breathless, but on the other side of the coin there was fear of losing if Abu Abad gets to know about this. So, she decided not to visit there because she doesn't want anything to happen again because she had suffered so many ruthless years under the dark and painful shade of her father.

Every morning Samar waited restlessly for Mariah, but she didn't come. He was upset and in fact he was missing her badly. He tried to get the information about Mariah, but people of the same village warned him to stay away from her.

"Love can cross any limit," Alee said.

"Yes, he too did, but without knowing the consequences," Responded Omar.

Finally, after long awaited day Samar met a guy in the woods who knows where Mariah lived and how her family reacts to this if ever, they get to know about it. So, wait was the only way out!

Chapter 6

Samar was there only for seven days tour, but he took the U-turn and decided to stay there forever. The guy whom he met told Samar everything about Mariah and how she became the victim of hatred and conflict. Samar felt heavy to hear about Mariah and his love for Mariah rose more and more.

The page on which he was going to write his first story remained half blanked as he didn't write more. He was lost in her thoughts and never had what he wanted to come out. He loved to stay there with the false appearance of Mariah.

"Humne Kaati Hain Tere Yaad Mein Ratein Aksar."

This line haunted Mariah more as she kept listening to this song whenever she find the time to tune to the radio station secretly without the consent of her father. She would lean against the ripped wall of her room with uncombed hair and kept thinking about that familiar touch of Samar.

Though both were strange to each other, but it seemed as if, their story is already written. She forgets the torture she had been through. Somehow, she could find herself in new place with new people holding the hand of Samar.

"If she didn't visit again then how they meet again," Alee questioned.

"As I told you when the hangover of true love attacks you and then no other force could restrict you from getting it." Replied Omar while looking at the dark orange light falling from the sun.

Samar conveyed a message to Mariah through that guy whom he met in the forests. He conveyed the same message to her, but he is the perfect guy who can be trusted. Meanwhile, Mariah thought that it is mandatory to meet Samar to tell him what is inside her heart. She was eager to reveal all her secrets, but to do that she was trying to know Samar more.

Finally, time came and they met at the same place where they happen to meet initially. Mariah was looking gorgeous! She had worn a knee length brown velvet dress followed by a traditional scarf called 'Hijab'. Samar was startled again to see her in that heavenly costume. He patted his heart to let it know that she is going to make an entry soon. He consoled his restless heart.

"How Samar was looking?" Alee questioned.

He was same like a muscle man with tall height resembling to his long silky and oily hair. His eyes were as bright as the shooting star. Over all they were looking alike in every aspect. It looked like they were made for each other.

Now, after exchange their eager gaze Samar began to talk to her, but at first, he stammered. He was not able to tell her about her name, likes and dislikes. He stammered like... "Wh...whh... whh... What is your name?" and the reply was

same with stammered voice like... "Ma... Ma... Ma... Mariah."
Now, slowly they began to talk freely and both were lost in
each other.

They kept talking and laughing all day long. It was the first
time Mariah was seen in that kind of mood. They were lost
in woods; they shared everything with each other.

Mariah shared every bit about her to Samar, but couldn't
express her love for Samar. In fact, Samar too didn't disclose
that she was his soul and love at first sight. The level of love
was above the danger mark. Gradually, they began to meet
daily and kept themselves busy in unending conversations.

Samar was sad to hear Mariah's struggle and the dark time
she had been through. He told Mariah that after marriage
they will run away from this valley of beasts. He hugged her
and she could hear his heart beats against his chest, she felt
that she will never think to live her life without Samar. Samar
had now become the part of her life and she doesn't want to
lose him at any cost.

Their love grew with time, but they never thought that it is
ephemeral and would fade away soon. Samar would rest his
head in her lap and sing 'Ghazals' for her. She would listen
and appreciate his voice and words. Both were happy as if
they knew each other since ages. Like flower blooms for
some time and then it gets withered either by the betrayal of
seasons or the unpredictable storms. Like water shows its
shine in the summer and becomes ice in winter.

Life is strange we even don't know what will happen next, but we keep trying to get to our unattained goal. If we talk about 'Snowdrop' it is the same brave flower that grows even in harsh winter; it penetrates through hard surface of snow and blooms, but that too only for some time and then the cruel winter squeezes it and shrank its roots to make it paralyzed? Then the flower never comes out again to rise like the undefeated kings. Winter is the only season that never realizes what love is and what life is? It kept pushing creatures to the limits and then in the end they either attempt suicide or gave up. Take the example of birds where do they go when they find no food and shelter. They either die of starvation or they get eaten up by other creatures. See, how hard life is in winters.

"What are you trying to say?" Alee said.

"It is something very horrible and painful that even a heartless person could weep and cry," Omar replied.

"What is that?"

"Listen, carefully."

"I am listening, just go on."

Samar had left everything behind to get the love of Mariah. He left his luxurious life, comfortable cars, bank full of money, his writing career etc. simply he renounced everything just for Mariah. But Mariah didn't have anything that she could give. She could have left her family, but then she would think about her mother Huzaifa.

Huzaifa was also the same victim of torture who was confined inside the four walled city. Her sons were same as their father; they never take good care of their old mother who fought bravely to raise them. They were disobedient; they had a good relation with their cruel father who was only cruel to Mariah and Huzaifa.

Mariah suddenly stopped visiting the green meadows of Murray. Samar kept visiting and he was waiting for Mariah, but Mariah never came back.

What!

"What happened with her?" Alee questioned in a shocking tune.

Yes, Mariah never came back even not for a single moment. She never showed her face to Samar, but she was watching everything what was happening and what is going to happen with Samar in future. She was afraid she sacrificed her love to save Samar. The guy whom Samar met and conveyed the same message to her father Abu Abad. He was enraged and he felt shame inside and he was impatient. That guy proved untrustworthy and it almost ruined life of Mariah and Samar.

Abu Abad, after hearing that Mariah had an affair with Samar; he began to beat her ruthlessly; It was Huzaifa again who tried to save Mariah, but all in vain. Mariah suffered so many head injuries. However, she had learnt how to endure this pain she was suffering from. She was unable to move; her feet's had swollen due to the blows of steel sticks; her back was as reddish as the color of blood. Her clothes were half ripped even he didn't spare her hair and chopped that off.

"How tyrannical he was!" Alee said with a thick tear in his eyes.

Don't cry my brother save those precious pearls because there is something more to come and then you will be given the freedom to cry. Abu Abad ordered his family to stop delivering food to Mariah. She was hungry for almost a week.

Those striking eyes were no longer that beautiful; she was more like skeleton with loose and fragile skin over it. Now, tears too stopped to come out from her dried eyes. There was only blood now flowing through her jaundiced eyes. Her face had turned yellowish and lips black and cracked.

Samar was feeling uneasy as he did not have any kind of information about Mariah. He was searching for Mariah like an insane lover. He too stopped to take food; he kept thinking about Mariah, but he was no longer in touch with her. He doesn't know her condition; he was screaming like an injured imprisoned lion. He searched the whole Maidan Soz, but couldn't find her. He was getting worse day by day.

Meanwhile, Abu Abad had sent his coward sons to teach him a lesson. They went to find Samar and cordoned the whole forest and started a profound massive search operation. Finally, they found him in a nearby hut. Hamad had an iron rod and he gave him a blow right on his back side and Ahmad lifted some wooden made jack hammer and smashed his head. The blood was oozing through his wounds; they kept beating him until he fell unconscious. They then left the place and went straight to their home and poured everything before Abu Abad. They thought that Samar is no more now. They thought, but he wasn't dead.

Chapter 7

Mariah was waiting for Samar. She would wake up and watch through the windows to see the glimpse of her ephemeral love. It is really heartbreaking how we let our women folks suffer and how we treat them. The pain she was going through was unimaginable and unbearable.

"You know, Alee, I was listening to the song from Laila Majnu movie. I was broken inside and couldn't stop my tears," Omar said.

"Doori Yeh Kam He Na Hou... Main Needun Main Be Chal Raha. Laakh Wade Jahan Ke Jhute Hain; Mere Houna Ahista Ahista."

I could somehow relate their story to Leila Majnu. Although this is different story, yet it has some resembling features. Samar was lost and he didn't find any way out to reach to the end. Finally, he decided to visit Mariah's house without knowing the cause. He went to find his love with blood stained clothes and body. He didn't even wipe away the blood from his head. How insane he was?

He kept walking throughout the night; having no fear in his mind. Ultimately, he reached his destination and slept on the main door of Abu Abad's house. In little morning Huzaifa saw someone who was sleeping on the main door. She called Abu Abad and asked her the same. Abu Abad was too failed to recognize him, but in the mean time his sons came in and they told their father that he was Samar. His face turned reddish and he again ordered his sons to throw him out of his house. He grabbed the collar of his ripped shirt and said, "You bastard, how dare you come here?" but his reply was heart throbbing.

"Let me meet Mariah only once. I can't live without her."

Huzaifa was weeping silently to hear those true words of Samar. Samar refused to runaway and he started screaming and crying her name. Suddenly, Mariah heard the noise and she went straight to the window and saw her brothers were dragging him. She cried 'Samar' so many times, but he was not able to hear her voice. She tried to open the door it was locked. She was frustrated she screamed loudly; she destroyed everything what was inside her room.

How painful!

Don't know where did Samar go after that, but Mariah was still locked. Her dry tears never stopped to fall. She could watch the memories of her short love story then she would laugh and weep. His appearance was killing her slowly. She had crossed the limits of insanity. Her mother couldn't do anything for her as she too was in the same prison.

Mariah had never expected that her brothers could perform such heinous acts. They were literate, but of no use. She thought that it is better to be illiterate than literate because they don't have the perfect sense to understand the situation. They savagely attacked Samar and bruised his inner peace and love. She was happy with what little knowledge she had. Months passed and Samar was no longer visible. Mariah searched the whole Maidan Soz, but couldn't find him. She had left her hope to rise again; she thought that Samar is dead like her hopes.

She was broken and she could only see Samar everywhere. Wherever she goes, she would call him. For some moments Mariah had thought that her barren life would rise again and she would live those lost moments of her life. She would cure those scars given by her father. But unfortunately nothing good happened with her. She was made for this and she accepted it happily. Now, Mariah kept visiting that place even in harsh winter. People would watch her singing 'Ballads' for her beloved. She was completely lost.

The cruel winter arrived again and again it showed its nature. Mariah was missing, nobody paid attention towards. Her father was happy to hear such good news. He heaved a sigh of relief.

"What about Samar?" Alee questioned.

"Somebody propagated the news that Samar is dead."

"Oh My Gosh! How?"

I am still confused was he dead or alive? Or was that the false news? Was it a pre-planned murder? I don't know, but it was terrible news for Mariah. The day she heard about Samar, she left home in the middle of the night holding a lantern to guide her. The climate was overcast and almost five feet snow had been recorded earlier. She didn't cared, but kept walking through the snow barefooted.

"I am amazed how did she survive?" Alee questioned.

"She didn't survive, but something bad was going to happen with her, though it was pre-planned," Answered Omar.

Huzaifa was mourning over the death of Samar and she put all the blame over Abu Abad and his ruthless sons. Now, she was searching for Mariah alone through the snow, but couldn't find her anywhere. She was crying, screaming because of the injustice they were facing. Mariah left her home to overcome the torture; nobody had thought that she would take such a big step.

After several days Abu Abad felt that he is missing his daughter. He felt restless and uneasy and began to enquire where Mariah is? Now, he realized that he had done a big mistake. He was worried and afraid of losing Mariah. He cursed himself of not loving his daughter.

He was in serious pain because he never felt anything like that before. It was the first time he began to miss his daughter. He recalled everything what he did with poor Mariah. That torture and those tears in fact he recalled everything. He was now desperate to see his daughter. His heart was not with him it was somewhere else.

One day in the middle of the night he went up and began to cry aloud. Huzaifa would console him and then he told

Huzaifa to wake up Hamad and Ahmad and said, "Let's go we will find her. I can't live without her."

They now started their journey towards the forest and many other people of the village were also with him. They made groups and began to search Mariah, but it was hard to walk through snow. They crossed hills, lanes, alleys almost everything, but couldn't find her. Hopeless Abu Abad failed to get Mariah. Earlier he failed to kill Mariah and this time he failed to get his daughter. This is life we should take decisions carefully; he was careless and tasted its bitterness. They returned hopelessly. He was crying inside so was Huzaifa.

In the morning he conveyed this message to the whole village and requested them to help him in finding her daughter. People were amazed to see Abu Abad worried about his daughter Mariah. They assembled and talked to Abu Abad about the matter and he explained everything before them. He confessed what he has done with that little Mariah. He was apologetic and there was sense of remorse in his every word. He promised his wife Huzaifa that he will find her out. It was the sunny day and the whole Maidan Soz was covered with white gleaming carpet (Snow) and whole valley was looking mesmerizing.

"So, finally he accepted his mistake," Alee said.

"Yes, then after that they started their search operation," Replied Omar.

After travelling miles and miles they didn't even have a little glimpse of Mariah. They followed the footsteps, but it would fade away when they were following those footsteps. Frustration, confusion was clearly visible on their remorseful and wrinkled faces.

Abu Abad began to call Mariah what he got was the echo of her name. The echo would slap him with the passing wind. He did a big mistake indeed. He was exhausted and couldn't walk more to find her, but this was the last hope and option to get Mariah and seek forgiveness.

Time changes everything and everyone and it changed Abu Abad too. He was sorry for everything what he did with his daughter, wife and the old Mukaram, his father. He never thought that he is father also and he might face the same torture. He was praying, pleading and requesting ALLAH to not take away Mariah from him. But destiny had something different for him. Everyone was searching for her calling with her name. 'Mariah... Mariah... Mariah...' but nothing returned back except the painful echoes.

Among them was that guy who helped Samar to get reach of Mariah told Abu Abad about her favorite place. Abu Abad rushed towards the place with his associates. Some of them were dummies and lose hearted and they couldn't walk much through the snow. Abu Abad was screaming and running towards the same place he was asked to visit. It took them two hours to reach their, though it was thirty minutes journey.

Abu Abad was yelling at himself; he even slapped his face. Sometimes he would collide with the hidden woods inside the snow in frustration and the people would come and help him out. He sensed something bad and his heart was beating indifferently.

"What was that?" Alee inquired.

"Just listen."

He was not able to control his fast heart beats. He fell unconscious, but still he was on his feet. He was eager to see his daughter, but what he saw was hard to bear.

Chapter 8

After reaching there on the spot they searched, but couldn't get her again. Abu Abad summoned the guy who knows where that place exactly is? He guided them towards the spot through the extremely dense forest. They went down though it was hard to find the exact location because everything was under the snow. But they managed to get there with lot of efforts.

The location was as peaceful as the sounds of birds in the morning. A little crystal clear stream was flowing through the forest and there were some beautiful trees around. They were amazed to see the hidden place that was chosen by Mariah. Everything was covered with snow.

Abu Abad was calling her daughter loudly, but he didn't receive any reply or response. He was broken inside. He was not able to control his tears. After so many calls his voice had turned hoarse and he took a refugee under a pine tree, leaned against it and was looking blankly at the sky with remorseful eyes. You know what he was sitting under the same tree where Mariah used to sit for all day long singing the songs of love and sorrow. Abu Abad has almost exhausted his ingenuity of find her, but he wasn't aware that she was on his opposite side covered with the blanket of frozen snow.

"What do you mean? Was she dead?" Alee asked.

"Listen carefully I told you, the story will unnerve you," Omar replied.

"It has already weakened my nerve. Now, what is next?" He responded.

The disaster was on the edge to destroy Abu Abad's will and ignorance. He earlier deprived Mariah from getting education and love of her life, but he was now feeling deprived. The unimaginable oppression and profound impact was about to kill him. He knew he was inhumane towards Mariah and this was the fruit he had sowed some decades ago for his evil deeds.

He was living with the illusion that Mariah is alive, but unfortunately, she was not. There was only feet distance between them; both were opposite to each other. One dead and one was alive, but he was a living corpse and dead inside. He was full of sleep while on the other side people kept searching for Mariah. They too had lost their hopes of finding her.

The vibrant mood was no longer visible; he was feeling low. He was brimming with negative thoughts and fear. After some time he stood up and turned around the tree slowly. He suddenly stumbled with something and then he fell down with face against the snow. He thought that it was the piece of wood he stumbled with. He ignored and wiped away the snow from his clothes reluctantly. He walked some steps then he went back and pushed the piece of wood. That was actually not a piece of wood, but the frozen corpse of Mariah.

He was shocked to see her; a loud painful shriek came out from his heart. He fell unconscious because what he saw was seriously unbearable. That beautiful lady was no longer in her charming posture. Her body was more like a decayed piece of flesh; her eyes had turned white and her face same as ashen. The hair she possessed was frozen like icicles. The people around rushed towards Abu Abad after hearing his heart wrenching scream. They too found that Mariah was dead.

Huzaifa held her daughter in her arms and hugged her tightly. She never knew that she is going to witness one of the most destructive days of her life. She cursed Abu Abad of not being a good father, she was all covered with snow.

"How painful and heart breaking. I can't imagine this," Alee said with teary eyes.

"I too cried a lot after hearing her story that's why I shared it with you," Replied Omar.

Abu Abad was unaware and he was not taking it seriously. In the end life gave him a befitting reply. He was seeking forgiveness, but could not forgive himself. He started his new life, but the remorse he was living with never faded away.

Every moment he would think about his daughter. He would curse himself. That ignorant, quizzical and stout Abu

Abad was now weak. He left everything and began to take care of his family. He was seeking forgiveness from Huzaifa, but she didn't. The fire inside her heart was raising more and more.

Many a times he told Huziafa; that he is really ashamed of what he has done with that little rose. He was totally changed; he used to spend more time on her grave than in his home. After morning prayers he would bring flowers and scatter on her grave proudly. He was proud of his daughter who never uttered a single word even after so many brutal attacks. He erected an epitaph and festooned her name on it. He decorated her graveyard with his own efforts and hard work.

The bereavement of Abu Abad lasted till his death, but the resistance of Mariah is still known in the valleys of Maidan Soz. His anguished thoughts and exasperating violence didn't let him live long. After many years he too departed from this world and left behind his wife and sons. The inseparable paradise turned into hell after the death of Mariah. Every side and every creature of the valley was quiet and silent as if they are still wailing over the death of Mariah.

"This is the first ever story that brought tears into my eyes." Alee said, "As a son, father, brother, husband I would never let any women down. I took this pledge before God and before you."

That's really great! You know what is the problem of our societies? They do the same what Abu Abad did. It is we who are responsible for everything. We suppress our women folks and reduce their value to zero. In fact, they too have that capability and potential to rise and achieve highest ranks in the society. But we are savages; we never let them enjoy the freedom that we have attained decades ago.

I guess we are entirely responsible because we are not able to visit such places to create awareness about women education. We should start a campaign and we should try to reach such places where these types of incidents took place every month. And they either attempt suicide or remain silent like suppressed slaves.

Women are the asset of every nation, but still we demoralize them and deprive them from everything. This is seriously a big threat for any nation. If we can't help them out, then who would? We need not only weapons, but a strong determination and with that we can achieve anything. Just began the campaign from village level; bring forth what they are lacking and what they need to do and to convince them that education is must for everyone.

The present world is digitalizing! So, we can't stay illiterate even in such facilities. Just teach them and train them to face any challenges. If we do so then no other Mariah would face the same torture and brutality. We need to educate them, no matter what it takes. For that we don't need political support and trust me politics is all crap. We can do it by ourselves because knowledge can be gained anywhere and there is no one who could snatch it away from us. The only thing is we need to come forward and act upon it.

"You are right. We should initiate such steps towards the betterment of women in our country," Alee said proudly.

People of Maidan Soz still hear the echoes and screams of Mariah. They often visit there and having said that she is still alive in the valleys of Maidan Soz; playing with the soul of Samar even if nobody has any kind of information about Samar. Was he dead or alive? Anyways, we consider him dead and may their souls rest in peace.

We hope to see a positive sign soon!

"Yes, we will do our best to bring the positivity elements in everyone."

Take care of yourself! Alee... See you soon with the next story because there is still much to explore!

To be continued...

You can contact the Publisher at:

www.fanatixx.in